243/2000 miles

I ♡ m you

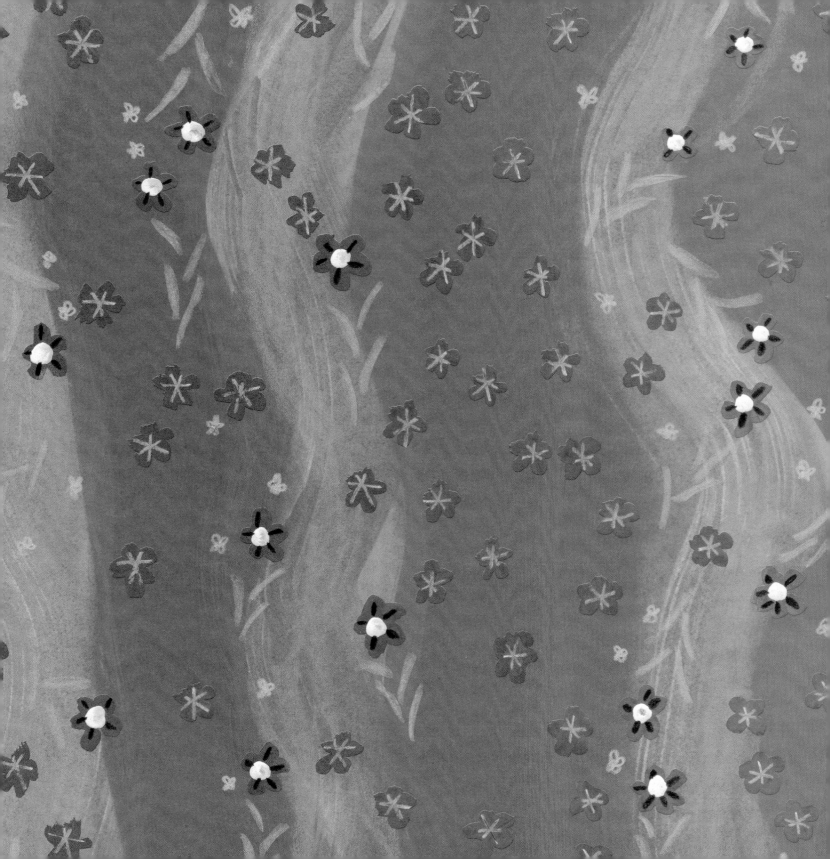

To Nathan and Naomi

D. K.

This book was
typeset in Berlonia.

Text copyright © 2016 by Dori Kleber.
Illustrations copyright © 2016 by G. Brian Karas.
All rights reserved. Published by Scholastic Inc., 557 Broadway, New York, NY 10012,
by arrangement with Candlewick Press.

ISBN-13: 978-1-338-15198-5
ISBN-10: 1-338-15198-3

4 5 6 7 8 9 10   40   25 24 23 22 21 20 19 18 17

More-igami

illustrated by
G. Brian Karas

Dori Kleber

SCHOLASTIC INC.

Joey loved things that folded.

He collected old road maps.

He played the accordion.

He slept in a foldaway bed.

One day, Sarah Takimoto's mother came to school.

She took a plain piece of paper.

She folded it,

and flipped it,

and pulled it,

until
it
became . . .

a crane.

Joey's eyes popped. His jaw dropped.
Mrs. Takimoto called it origami.

"I want to make origami," Joey told her.
"Will you teach me?"

"I can show you the folds," she said,
"but if you want to be an origami master,
you'll need practice and patience."

Joey started that afternoon. He practiced on his notebook paper and on the construction paper from the art shelf. But even his simple shapes were crooked and crumpled.

So he practiced on his homework . . .

and on the newspaper . . .

and on his sister's
sheet music.

And he practiced on
all the gift wrap . . .

and on the recipe
for Aunt Vivian's
pineapple surprise . . .

and on the thirty-eight dollars in Mom's purse.

"This folding has to stop," said Mom.

Joey drooped. How would he ever become an origami master without practice?

He went next door to Muy Mexicana.
Fajitas always made him feel better.

"Joey!" Mr. Lopez sang. "Hey, what's wrong?"

"It takes practice and patience to be an origami master," Joey said. "But whenever I practice, everybody else loses their patience."

"Many artists are misunderstood, *amigo*," said Mr. Lopez. "Especially when they are just learning."

"What's that?" Mr. Lopez asked, pointing to Joey's napkin.
"A pyramid," said Joey. "Sorry."
"No, don't apologize," Mr. Lopez said. "I like it.
It makes the table look fancy. Could you make more?"
Joey grinned. "I could make a hundred!"

So Joey folded and folded and folded until pyramids perched on every table in the restaurant.

Each day after school, Joey went back to Muy Mexicana. He folded napkins into fans.

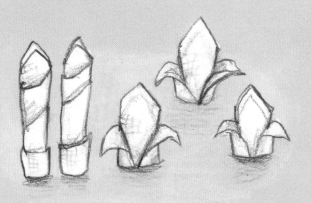

He made candlesticks. Then he tried crowns.

Some napkins toppled. Others flopped. But Joey kept folding until they were perfect.

Finally, he was ready to try the most difficult fold of all.

He took a crisp napkin.

He folded.

He flipped.

He pulled.

It worked! A crane!

At last, he was an origami master.

Just then, a girl walked in. She was waving a paper fan. Her eyes popped. Her jaw dropped.

"Did you make that?" she asked.
Joey nodded.

"I can show you how," said Joey.
"But I should warn you. It takes
practice—and lots of patience!"

Fold your own origami ladybug

Are you ready to make origami? Try this ladybug.

Keep practicing until it's just right!

1. Start with a square piece of paper. Fold it in half to make a triangle.

2. Fold the triangle in half. Press down hard to make a crease, then open it back up.

3. Now fold the top corners down so they reach a little past the bottom edge of the paper. Leave some space around the center crease.

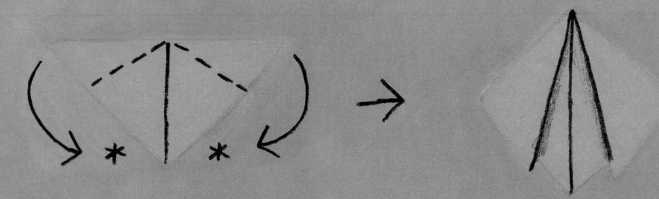

4. Flip the paper over. Fold the top corner down to the center of your paper.

5. Then fold the point of that same corner back up, so it hangs over the top of the paper.

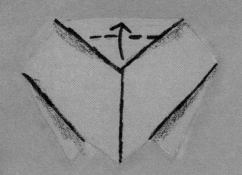

6. Flip the paper over again. Add some spots to the wings to make it look like a real ladybug.

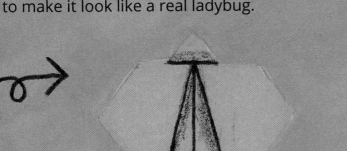

You did it!